# THE HOUSE

RAELYN DRAKE

darbycreek
MINNEAPOLIS

Darby Creek
A division of Lerner Publishing Group, Inc.
241 First Avenue North
Minneapolis, MN 55401 USA

For reading levels and more information, look up this title at www.lernerbooks.com.

Cover and interior images: AlenKadr/Shutterstock.com (texture); iStock.com/Vectorfactory (skyline); iStock.com/yanka444 (bricks); iStock.com/Nataly-Nete (window).

Main body text set in Janson Text LT Std 12/17.5.
Typeface provided by Adobe Systems.

**Library of Congress Cataloging-in-Publication Data**

Names: Drake, Raelyn, author.
Title: The house / Raelyn Drake.
Description: Minneapolis : Darby Creek, [2018] | Series: Mason Falls mysteries | Summary: On a dare, Grace, Kat, and Damien agree to spend an hour in a house rumored to be haunted, and their scientific investigation reveals hidden truths.
Identifiers: LCCN 2017029165 | ISBN 9781541501133 (lb) | ISBN 9781541501171 (pb) | ISBN 9781541501188 (eb pdf)
Subjects: | CYAC: Haunted houses—Fiction. | Mystery and detective stories.
Classification: LCC PZ7.1.D74 Hou 2018 | DDC [Fic]—dc23

LC record available at https://lccn.loc.gov/2017029165

Manufactured in the United States of America
1-43785-33637-9/1/2017

TO MY SISTER AINA:
"IT'S LOCKED!"

# CHAPTER 1

As Grace Levine stared at the house, she could've sworn it stared right back at her. The house at the end of her block looked as run-down and empty as it always had. Even Grace's mother had warned her to stay away from the place. Not that her mother believed in ghosts any more than Grace herself did, but the abandoned house had a creepy reputation among the residents of Mason Falls.

Grace paused with her hand on the rusty iron gate and turned to her friends, Kat Tanaka and Damien Smith. "You guys ready?" she asked.

"Of course!" Damien said, adjusting his gear bag on his shoulder. "Those ghosts won't stand a chance against our thorough scientific investigation."

"There's only one ghost, according to legend," Grace pointed out. "Cordelia Rose."

Kat looked less sure than the rest of them, especially at the mention of Cordelia Rose. "I thought she was a witch," she said, twisting the end of her braid around her finger.

"No, she wasn't a witch," Grace said.

"I've heard it both ways," Damien said.

"She was a famous medium in the 1920s," Grace explained. "Supposedly, she could get in touch with the spirits of the dead. And now her ghost haunts this house. At least that's how the story goes."

"We don't have to go in," Kat whispered. "We can just tell Hector and Chrissy that we completed their stupid dare."

Damien shook his head. "They'll totally know if we don't spend the whole hour in there. In fact, they're probably watching us right now."

Grace looked uneasily over her shoulder at the deserted street. Cars passed occasionally on the main road a block away, but Cherry Avenue was a dead end.

It was tradition at Mason Falls High for the seniors to choose a few underclassmen each year and dare them to spend one hour in the old house on Cherry Avenue. If you made it through the hour, you got special privileges like sitting with the seniors at lunch. If you failed, the seniors would tell everyone in the school that you were a cowardly crybaby.

This year Grace and her friends were chosen. At first they had been tempted to ignore the challenge—for one thing, they saw sitting with people like Hector Rodriguez and Chrissy Boyd at lunch as more of a chore than a reward. But then they realized that they had a unique opportunity to make a change at their school. They had spent all week brainstorming, and now they were ready to put their plan into action.

"We need to get proof that shows everyone at school that the house isn't haunted," Grace reminded them. "And the only way to do that is to explore the house."

"But what if the house *is* haunted?" Kat asked.

"It isn't," Damien said.

"But what if it *is*?" she repeated.

Grace pulled her gaze away from her family's house on the corner, where jack-o'-lanterns smiled from the porch and orange string lights twinkled cheerfully in the dark. "Even if it is haunted—which I kinda doubt—we don't have to tell Hector and Chrissy the truth. The important thing is ending this stupid tradition once and for all."

She looked back at the house and pushed her glasses up her nose with a determined half smile.

"Let's do this."

/////

The iron gate opened soundlessly. Grace frowned. "I was expecting it to open with a screeching sound."

Damien shrugged and pushed past her. Kat followed, her flashlight trained on the stone path that led to the front steps. Grace pulled the gate shut behind them.

The gate may have been quiet, but the stairs creaked and groaned loudly as they climbed the three steps to the front porch.

"What's that?" Kat asked, shining her flashlight on an object near the door.

Damien raised an eyebrow. "It looks like—"

"A candy bowl," Grace finished. "Like someone left out candy for trick-or-treaters." She bent down to look more closely. The bowl was shaped like a witch's cauldron, but the brightly colored candy inside looked normal enough. It also looked modern and wasn't caked with dust like everything else seemed to be. Grace reached a hand into the bowl.

"Don't touch it," Kat hissed. "That's how witches lure you in."

Grace rolled her eyes. "I'm just collecting evidence." The wrapper crinkled as she stuck a chocolate bar in her backpack.

Damien pulled out his phone. "Did everyone remember to charge their phones?"

"Yep," Grace said, "and the night vision camera I ordered is good to go." She retrieved the device from her backpack.

"Can I do the EVP recordings?" Kat asked. "That's the one where I get to ask the ghost questions, right?"

Damien nodded. "It stands for Electronic Voice Phenomenon. You use that app you downloaded to record, but in theory we won't be able to hear if the ghost replies until we play back the recording later."

"I'll use the night vision camera to record video of everything we see," Grace added. "We'll have the flashlight, but otherwise it's going to be pitch black in there."

"Don't remind me," Kat said, shuddering.

Grace tried to peer in through windows, but a coating of grime and yellowed lace curtains blocked her view.

A heavy padlock was bolted to the front door. A sign underneath read:

*PRIVATE PROPERTY*

*KEEP OUT*

"How are we supposed to get past this?" Grace asked, but as she reached out to grab it, the padlock twisted in her hand. Someone had filed through the metal loop, but it was impossible to tell unless you looked closely.

Grace slid the padlock out of the latch and placed it carefully on the porch next to the door, looking again to make sure the coast was clear. It was common knowledge that the house had been empty for years, but she wasn't sure if anyone still bothered to check on it.

She looked at the clock on her phone. They had timed it perfectly, 9:00 p.m. exactly.

"Okay, guys, we just have to last until ten o'clock, and we complete the dare. Then back to my house for snacks and movies."

"No big deal," Damien said.

"Yeah, no big deal," Kat echoed, sounding more confident than she looked.

They pushed open the front door and went inside.

/////

They found themselves inside a cramped, dark hallway that stretched from the door to the back of the house. Kat darted the beam of her flashlight around the room. Grace pulled the front door closed behind her but left it open just a crack—a thin sliver of moonlight to remind them that there was always a way out. But Grace wasn't about to let Hector Rodriguez and Chrissy Boyd think that she was too scared to stay in an old house for an hour. There was no such thing as ghosts, and they were going to prove it. Grace tried not to imagine the very real things that could be lurking in the darkness, like rats and spiders.

She looped the handle of the small night vision camera over her hand. The night vision made everything look gray, instead of green like she had expected. Damien's and Kat's eyes were glowing points of light.

Directly ahead of them, a set of stairs climbed to the second floor, disappearing into shadow. Immediately to their left was some sort of formal sitting room, dining room on their right, and farther down the hall was the kitchen—if the stories of other teens who had braved the house were to be trusted.

They all spoke in whispers.

"This one guy at school," Kat began, "told me there are shelves of jars filled with eyeballs and frogs and stuff. That's why people say Cordelia was a witch."

Grace grimaced. "We'll see for ourselves soon enough."

"Should we stick together or split up?" Damien asked.

Grace shook her head. "It never, *ever* works out well when people split up to explore haunted houses."

Kat snorted. "Split up? I'm not letting you two out of my sight." She jiggled the beam of her flashlight across the faded wallpaper in nervous zigzags as she spoke.

"Besides," Grace said, "the paranormal investigation thing was our idea. It wasn't part of the dare. Splitting up to cover more ground won't make our hour pass any faster."

"We do want to make sure we get enough evidence, though," Damien pointed out. "Should we start in the sitting room?"

/////

The old floorboards shifted under their feet as they made their way into the first room. A thick layer of dust coated everything. Grace held a finger under her nose to keep from sneezing. A fireplace dominated one end of the room, the mantle and the wall above it stained with soot. Chairs and end tables seemed to crouch here and there, casting odd shadows on the walls when the flashlight hit them.

The chair nearest to Grace had once been covered in velvet upholstery, but now it was age-rotted and sun-faded. Grace wondered how enough light had ever made its way inside this gloomy house.

Kat shone her flashlight along the top of the mantle. It was lined with an assortment of dusty metal candle holders, cracked vases filled with dried roses, and ceramic figurines that may have been pretty at one time but were so crusted over with cobwebs that it wasn't even clear what they were supposed to be.

Kat wrinkled her nose. "I would have thought that when the last owners moved out, they would have taken all of their furniture and stuff."

"Who was the last person to live here anyway?" Damien asked.

Grace frowned, considering the question. "I don't know, actually. I guess it couldn't have been Cordelia Rose because she lived here almost a hundred years ago, and someone must have lived here after that."

"The house was already empty when my parents were kids," Damien said. "My dad says it's always been abandoned and it's always been haunted." His voice trailed off as the wind picked up outside, whistling under the doors and rattling the windows. Thunder rumbled ominously in the distance.

Kat groaned. "If I had known it was going to be a dark and stormy night, I would never have agreed to this, dare or no dare."

Grace lifted the edge of the yellowed lace curtain and peered out through the dirty window as rain began to spatter on the glass.

"How long has it been?" Kat asked.

Grace's mouth quirked. "Since we got here? Five minutes."

Kat sighed. "Well, let's start collecting evidence. I need something to keep my mind off the storm outside and the spider I thought

I saw in the corner." She opened the EVP app on her phone.

Grace held up the night vision camera and started to record a video.

"Are there any spirits here with us that would like to communicate?" Kat asked.

They all held their breath, listening.

After a pause, Kat added. "I invite you to come talk with us. We mean you no harm."

Damien snickered. "Yeah, we come in peace," he muttered. "Take us to your leader."

Kat elbowed him. "Do you have a name?" she asked. "What's your name?"

If something was answering Kat's questions, none of them could hear it. Kat looked at Grace and shrugged.

Grace stepped closer to where Kat held her phone and asked, "Can you give us a sign of your presence?"

The door flew shut behind them.

# CHAPTER 2

Damien yelped and Kat jumped. Grace's heart pounded.

"What was that?" Grace asked, even though she had seen the door close. She ran over and yanked it open. The hallway was empty.

"My phone just turned off!" Kat exclaimed. "I think the battery's dead."

"I told you to charge it before we left," Damien chided.

"I did!" Kat protested. "It was fully charged, I swear. But the screen went black and now it won't turn back on." She jabbed at the power button desperately. "I've heard this happens when a spirit tries to appear. The ghost draws on the nearest source of power. In this case, my phone's battery."

Grace seriously doubted that a ghost had drained Kat's phone battery, but she had to admit that it was a bit of an odd coincidence. She checked her own phone's battery. It was still near full power. "Hopefully the EVP recordings saved properly," she said. "We can access them later when we plug in your phone."

"Either way, that definitely seemed like a sign," Kat said, a slight tremble in her voice.

"It could have been the wind," Damien said, sounding like he was trying to convince himself as well as his friends. "We left the front door open a crack, and the storm is picking up outside."

"Yeah, I guess so," Kat said.

Grace took a few breaths to calm her rapid pulse. "So, kitchen next, I guess?" she suggested, trying to ignore the nervous twisting of her stomach.

"Lead the way," Damien said.

Grace glared at him as they headed into the hallway and toward the back of the house.

There were a few other doors scattered along the hallway, but most of them were locked when Grace or the others tried to open them.

Kat sniffed as she passed her flashlight's beam from door to door. "It smells in here."

"Well, what do you expect?" Grace questioned. "It's an old, abandoned house. All the wood is old and decaying. And it's not like anyone has been cleaning in here over the past few decades."

"I guess." Kat shrugged.

"I actually thought it would be worse," Damien said. "I thought the place would be filled with, like, animal nests in the corners."

Grace scoffed. "Are you seriously complaining about the lack of animal nests?"

"Maybe the animals know better than to come in here," Kat whispered. "Because they know *something* is already in here."

Damien rolled his eyes.

Lightning flashed outside, filling the dark hallway with a blinding white light. The boom of thunder that followed a split second later shook the windowpanes with its deep bass rumble. Grace thought she could hear Kat muttering under her breath about the storm. Grace usually loved storms, at least when she could watch them from the safety of her family's screened-in front porch with a cup of hot cocoa and her cat, Pixel, curled up in her lap. She could see why so many horror and ghost stories took place at night during storms. The fact that Halloween was only two days away only added to the spooky atmosphere.

They reached the kitchen, which was just as dust coated as everything else they had seen so far. It was an old-fashioned space. An icebox or a sink with a pump wouldn't have looked out of place. But instead there was a yellowed fridge and matching electric stove. Two windows above the sink looked out over the backyard. The curtains were open on these windows, and the lightning flickered like a strobe light, throwing strange shadows against the walls.

Kat aimed her flashlight at the shelves that lined part of the room. "What are those things?"

Grace went to look at them more closely. They looked like jars for canning jams or applesauce, like her grandma made. But they were filled with cloudy liquid, and the things floating in them did not look like canned peaches. She stepped back with a noise of disgust.

"I think they're eyeballs."

Damien snorted. "They are not!" He picked one up and looked at it. Grace could see the spheres bobbing in the liquid, and in the next flash of lightning, she could see the brightly colored irises contrasted against the white organs. Damien shoved the jar back on the shelf with a yelp, nearly dropping it. He wiped his hands frantically on his pants as though he had touched the eyeballs themselves. "What sort of creep keeps eyeballs in their kitchen?"

Kat moaned. "A witch, that's who!" She grabbed Grace by the shoulders and shook her. "I thought you said Cordelia Rose was a medium in the 1920s? I imagined a glamorous woman with a crystal ball and a fake accent, not a fairy tale witch with warts making potions out of frog legs and bat wings."

"She *was* a medium!" Grace protested, swatting Kat's hands away. "People came from all around to have their fortunes told by her. She grew so fabulously wealthy that some people began to suspect that she was a fake. Even Harry Houdini tried to expose her as a fraud—" Grace paused. She had heard what sounded like footsteps upstairs. But the wind was howling so loudly outside and the thunder rumbled angrily. Maybe she had imagined it. Her mom, who did volunteer work for the Mason Falls Historical Society, had explained that old houses tended to be noisy. They creaked as the foundation settled or as the wood expanded and contracted with age and temperature.

Kat and Damien seemed to have heard the footsteps as well. They both looked up at the ceiling warily for a moment. Then Kat turned back to Grace and said, "Harry Houdini? You mean the illusionist?"

"Yeah," Grace answered. "Harry Houdini performed magic tricks, but he never tried to pretend that he could really do magic. He was always up front about the fact that everything he did was all an illusion. And he hated that mediums and psychics took people's money in return for false hope, like promising they could communicate with lost loved ones. So he made it his mission to hunt down the fakes. His investigation of Cordelia Rose ruined her career, and she died in poverty."

Damien and Kat were both staring at her with wide eyes.

"How do you know all that?" Kat asked.

"I read it on this website about famous haunted places. There wasn't anything on Mason Falls, except a paragraph about Cordelia Rose and this house."

Damien sighed in exasperation. "You read it on a website? How do you even know that's legit?"

Grace pouted. "It was about as legit as any other paranormal website. I don't know if it's all true, but it's what we've got to go on at the moment."

"Well, witch or not, it's still creepy," said Damien.

Grace checked her phone and groaned. "Well, we still have half an hour to kill if we're going to beat this dare. So we might as well keep investigating."

Kat grimaced. "Don't say we have time to *kill*. This isn't a great time for that expression."

All of them avoided looking at the sitting room to their left as they started up the stairs. They were halfway up when a sound made them pause.

"Is that music?" Kat whispered.

Grace could hear the faint melody. It sent a crawling sensation down her spine.

# CHAPTER 3

They continued up the stairs, trying to stay quiet, but the stairs creaked loudly. The hallway at the top of the stairs ran parallel to the street outside. There was a door at the right end of the hallway and two doors on the left. Grace tried the one on the right, but it was locked.

The music grew louder as they approached the first door on the left, but it was hard to tell exactly where it was coming from. Damien carefully pushed the door open. It was a bedroom. Kat's flashlight beam hit the bed, and then they saw a shadowy figure that made them jump. Kat bit back a yelp. Even when

Grace realized that it was just a dressmaker's dummy in the corner, her heart wouldn't stop pounding.

"I'm beginning to wonder if ending this tradition is worth it," Damien grumbled, putting two fingers to his neck to feel his pulse.

"Oh sure, *now* you admit this was a ridiculous idea," Kat muttered under her breath.

"That's the whole point," Grace argued, ignoring Kat. "If we can prove the house isn't haunted, then no one else has to deal with this stupid dare ever again."

In this room, it was clear that the music was coming from the floor above.

"I feel like I have to draw the line somewhere," Kat said. "Can we *not* go up to the creepy haunted attic?"

"And do what?" Damien asked. "Just sit here?"

"We could wait in the bedroom," Kat suggested. She peered into the dark room. "It looks like there's some cool vintage makeup brushes and perfume bottles on the dresser—"

There was a loud thumping noise from behind them. They spun around. It seemed to be coming from the first floor. They couldn't see anything but the front door from this angle, but it almost sounded like someone walking with slow, steady steps down the hallway from the kitchen toward the front of the house where the stairs were.

The thumping came again, louder this time. Grace thought it sounded like someone slapping their hand against the hallway walls. Or was it just her imagination?

Then the sound stopped, and the silence that followed was somehow worse than the thumping sound had been.

They listened intently for several breathless moments, but all they could hear was the muted howl of wind from the storm outside.

"Hey, I have an idea," Kat said in a strangled whisper, "why don't we go check out the attic?"

They found the attic behind the second door at the left end of the hallway. The attic at Grace's house was a trap door in the ceiling with a pull-down ladder, but here the attic had its own rickety staircase. The music grew louder as they climbed. It sounded like old-timey jazz.

The attic was empty except for a phonograph, which stood playing in the middle of the room.

"I'm pretty sure that's music from the 1920s," Grace said.

"Cordelia Rose's time," Kat whispered.

Damien stared at the phonograph. "Wait, guys, don't you have to start these things by hand? My uncle has a vinyl collection and a record player, and I've seen him move the needle to start the record playing."

Grace gasped. "But that means—"

"Who started the record?" Kat finished.

"And why is it just sitting in the middle of the floor by itself?" Damien wondered.

Kat shone her flashlight into all the corners. Plenty of cobwebs, but there didn't seem to be anything else in the attic. Grace took a step forward toward the phonograph, and nearly shrieked when she walked straight into a cobweb in the dark.

"Oh yuck," she said, trying to get it out of her hair.

"There's no spiders in your hair, if that's what you're wondering," Damien said.

"This is why we're friends—you knew exactly what I was going to ask."

The record began to skip, looping the music in a jerky repetition of shrieking horn and static hiss.

"This whole place is straight out of a horror movie," Damien muttered.

"Our time has to almost be up, right?" Kat asked. She ran the end of her braid along her chin, and Grace knew her friend was fighting a nervous habit from her childhood of chewing on the end of her braid.

Grace shook her head. "Sorry, twenty minutes left."

Kat closed her eyes, eyebrows scrunched together, and then took a deep breath. She opened her eyes as she blew it out in a long sigh. "Okay," she said in an overly calm voice, her face suddenly turning serene. "I can handle this. I'm not going to lose my cool over a silly old house. If I can handle the opening night of a play with the stomach flu, then I can handle this."

"That's the spirit!" Damien said, clapping her on the back.

"Spirit?" Kat repeated. "Seriously, we need to work on our choice of words when we do things like this."

"Well, since you're so cool and calm now, can we go explore Cordelia Rose's bedroom on the second floor?" Damien asked.

The record stopped skipping and the song continued. The jaunty melody was a jarring contrast with the rasping, echoing sound of the old recording and the dark gloom of the attic. Somehow, it was more unsettling than a horror movie soundtrack.

"This attic is even creepier than the downstairs," Grace said.

Kat shuddered. "Yeah, let's go," she said, already heading back down the attic stairs.

The bedroom was more spacious than it had looked from the doorway. A bed with four posters and musty curtains stood at one end.

"Ooo, look over there!" Kat said, pointing with her flashlight.

On the other side of the room was a sitting area near glass doors that led to the balcony. Several ornate chairs surrounded the table. A moth-eaten embroidered tablecloth draped over the sides and hung all the way to the floor. Kat's flashlight beam glinted off a transparent sphere that sat on the table, surrounded by a circle of tarot cards.

"Is that a crystal ball?" Damien asked.

"It looks like one," Kat said. "Although it's hard to tell under all this dust." She carefully rubbed the dust off the globe with the arm of her sweatshirt. She wrinkled her nose when the dust left grimy streaks on the sleeve.

"That's definitely a crystal ball," Grace said. "I wonder if this is where Cordelia Rose used to hold séances."

"So this is where she would channel the spirit of the deceased," Kat said quietly.

"I think you mean 'where she pretended to contact the dead,'" Damien said.

Grace was quiet for a moment. Her throat prickled at the idea of being able to hear her dad, who had died five years ago. To get a message from him, even a single word, would mean everything. She swallowed the lump in her throat.

Without a word, Kat gave Grace a little side hug, as though she knew what Grace had been thinking about.

"Did you guys see that?" Damien asked suddenly. "I swear the crystal ball just lit up."

"Is there a light inside?" Grace asked. She couldn't see any sort of light bulb.

"Switch off your flashlight, Kat," Damien said. "It's too bright to tell."

Kat groaned but she switched it off anyway. Sure enough, the crystal ball was emitting a faint glow. It shone on the tarot cards arranged on the table, and Grace shuddered when she saw the grinning skeleton on one of the cards.

Kat moved toward one of the chairs.

"What are you doing?" Damien asked, sounding as surprised as Grace felt.

Kat took a seat at the séance table. "I think we should attempt to contact the ghost of Cordelia Rose."

# CHAPTER 4

"Let me get this straight," Damien said. "First you're complaining about how it was a bad idea to come here in the first place, and now you want to call the ghost?"

Kat picked up a few tarot cards and examined them. "Look, I'm just as creeped out as you are, but we can't leave yet or we lose the dare. Cordelia Rose was once a person just like us—"

Damien snorted. "Speak for yourself—"

"And," Kat continued, "I think she deserves a chance to tell her side of the story. If she really was a medium, then she'll know how to contact us."

Grace sighed. "That's a sweet thought, Kat, but—"

"And what better way to collect evidence?" Kat added. "If nothing happens, then that helps us prove that the house isn't haunted."

Grace had known Kat long enough to know that it was pointless to argue with her over any idea she was so passionate about.

Damien had to know that too, but that didn't mean he wasn't going to grumble about it. "This still seems like a terrible idea," he said as he sat down at the table. The chair cushion sent up a puff of dust that made him cough.

"I thought you didn't believe in ghosts," Kat asked him sarcastically.

Damien rolled his eyes. "I don't. I just think that anything we see or hear during a séance is going to be bogus because we'll just be seeing what our minds are expecting to see. The human brain is really good at imagining things that aren't there."

"That's what all this is for," Grace reminded him, setting up the night vision camera in the middle of the table. "We can't trust our eyes, but if Kat really does make contact with the ghost of Cordelia Rose, then we'll have proof that it wasn't just our imagination, right?"

Damien nodded reluctantly, then looked alarmed when Kat grabbed his hand.

Kat laughed at his confusion. "We have to sit around the table in a circle and hold hands."

"So suddenly you're an expert on séances?" Damien asked.

"I've seen a lot of movies," Kat muttered, as Grace sat next to her and joined hands with her and Damien, completing the circle.

Grace didn't feel any different, though she noticed that the storm had picked up outside. And also that Damien's hand was warm. She worried that her palms might start sweating, but she tried to push that thought out of the way. If this was going to be a proper investigation, then she was going to keep an open mind. Even when Houdini had exposed fake mediums, he always went to the séances ready and willing to be proven wrong. Desperately *hoping* to be proven wrong, actually. Houdini had admitted that he would give almost anything to be able to talk to his departed mother one more time.

Kat closed her eyes, the light coming from the crystal ball giving an eerie glow to her face like candlelight. Kat began to chant something—Grace was pretty sure that it was just the French folk song they had learned in choir last year. But Kat was a natural show-woman and in the dark gloom of the musty bedroom, it fit the mood perfectly. Grace suppressed a small shiver as thunder crackled outside. She was beginning to see how Cordelia Rose's clients would be able to believe that she really had the ability to contact spirits on the other side.

Kat stopped chanting. "We gather here," she said in her most dramatic voice, "to seek out any spirits of the departed. If you are there, O Spirits, we invite you to pierce the veil of death and—*ow!*"

Kat glared at Damien, who smirked, and Grace realized that he had kicked Kat under the table.

"Guys, c'mon. Damien, let Kat do this. And Kat, maybe ease up a little bit on the theatrics."

Kat pouted, but when she closed her eyes, she continued in her normal voice. "If there are any ghosts who wish to communicate with us, could you please give us another sign? Especially if Cordelia Rose is there. No offense to any ghosts who aren't Cordelia Rose, but we kinda came here to talk to her specifically."

Grace fought the urge to kick Kat under the table herself.

After a moment of what looked like intense concentration, Kat opened her eyes and peeked around the room to see if anything was happening.

Nothing was happening.

"Well," Damien said, "that was fun, but we only have to stay here for another ten minutes, so let's go take some more photos and get outta here—"

The door slammed shut behind them with a heart-stopping bang, just like it had downstairs in the sitting room. But before they even had a chance to process this, a loud shriek filled the air. The light coming from the crystal ball on the table turned blue and began to pulse. The table itself shook violently, rocking back and forth. They leaped to their feet, knocking their chairs to the floor. The high-pitched wail continued, making it hard to think straight. It sounded like a woman screaming, and it made Grace feel like screaming too.

A rational thought managed to wriggle through her panic. *We need evidence*, she thought.

She grabbed the night vision camera from the rattling séance table and made sure it was still recording. She spun in a circle, trying to get her bearings and make sure nothing was sneaking up behind her. It was hard to keep the camera steady when her hands were trembling.

Kat had grabbed on to Damien's arm and was breathing in shallow, panicked gasps. Damien yanked on the door handle. "It's locked!" he yelled, his eyes wide.

"We're trapped?" Kat asked, her voice rising to a squeak at the end.

Grace thought about the glass doors. They led to the second-floor balcony, which was directly above the front porch. Maybe they would be able to climb down to the porch using one of the columns that supported the balcony. Or jump straight from the second story into the bushes below if they had to. Jumping was a last resort, but a broken ankle was better than whatever was happening to them now.

All these thoughts raced through Grace's mind as she spun toward the window.

When she saw the ghost, she nearly dropped the camera, and all of her rational plans for escape were swallowed up by terror.

Cordelia Rose stood on the balcony, just visible through the grimy glass of the doors.

# CHAPTER 5

It was hard to make out details in the dark, but between the blue light from the crystal ball and the flickering lightning outside, Grace could see the figure in the knee-length beaded dress. Where her eyes should be, Grace could only see glowing white light. Her short, dark hair was plastered to her face in the rain. She pointed at the door with one thin arm, and the balcony doors burst open.

Grace really did scream that time. She felt Kat grab her hand and pull her through the door to the hallway, which Grace realized had opened at the same time as the balcony doors.

They pounded down the stairs, Damien close behind them. They tumbled through the front door and onto the front porch.

They ran as fast as they could down the block, sneakers slapping on the pavement as they headed back to Grace's house. Grace's mind was filled with the primal fear that something might be following them. Her only concern was putting as much distance between them and the house as they could.

She had never been so happy to reach the front steps of her house. It dawned on Grace that they would have to admit defeat to Hector and Chrissy since they had chickened out on the dare ten minutes early. Now that they were safe, Grace was a little embarrassed at how scared she had been.

"That you, Grace?" her mom called from the kitchen as they burst through the front door.

They exchanged worried glances as they paused in the foyer to take off their shoes. Grace had told her mom that she and Damien and Kat would be going to the movies and that they wouldn't get home until after 10:00.

But now they were soaked from the rain and covered in dirt and grime from the house. Her mom would never believe them.

"How'd the haunted house visit go?" her mom asked as they tramped into the kitchen. "You look like you've seen a ghost."

Grace's mouth hung open for a second. "What?" she asked.

"How do you know about that, Mrs. Levine?" Kat blurted out. Damien elbowed her.

Grace's mom snorted. "It's a couple of days before Halloween and your 'trip to the movies' mysteriously involves all-black clothes, your backpacks, and the ghost hunter supplies that Grace bought on the Internet last week? Of *course* you're going to go visit the haunted house down the block."

Grace spluttered. "But I—"

Her mom winked at them. "Just because you use your own money doesn't mean I don't get shipping notifications for my shopping account."

Kat snickered.

Grace's mom filled the electric kettle and switched it on. "So, how'd it go? If you tell me all the spooky details, I'll make you guys some hot cocoa."

They sat around the kitchen table, sipping hot cocoa and wrapping their chilled hands around the warm mugs.

"Now, who dared you?" Grace's mom asked. "I'm assuming this is part of the tradition where the seniors try to scare the underclassmen."

"You know about the dare?" Kat asked, eyes wide.

Grace's mom raised an eyebrow. "I wasn't in high school *that* long ago, Kat. The dare was already a tradition when Grace's father and I went there."

Kat blushed and smiled sheepishly.

"Yeah, it was these seniors—Hector Rodriguez and Chrissy Boyd," Grace explained. "We thought that if we could prove that the place wasn't really haunted, then we could put an end to the yearly dare. And, you know, make Hector and Chrissy look bad in the process," she muttered into her cocoa.

"And what did you guys find out?" her mom asked.

Grace sighed. "I'm not sure."

Damien shrugged, "I hate to admit it, but it seemed like the place might really be haunted."

Kat nodded enthusiastically. "Definitely haunted."

"Really?" Grace's mom asked.

Grace sighed. "Of course we were skeptical—"

"Speak for yourself," Kat said.

"But we saw some things that defy a logical explanation." Grace shuddered when she thought of the ghost.

"You recorded evidence, right?" Her mom pointed at their backpacks. "I assume that's what the night vision camera was for."

"Yep, and I downloaded some 'paranormal investigator' software, so we'll upload everything to our computers."

"Well," her mom said, "what you *saw* seemed to show that it was haunted, but maybe there's more to it than meets the eye. You should examine your recordings and photos and see if anything just doesn't add up."

"You're not going to tell us that it's *not* haunted?" Damien asked.

Grace's mom shrugged. "I'm a skeptic, but there's an awful lot of weird stories about that place. It was already abandoned when I was your age. I never had the guts to sneak in there, but Grace's father did the dare. He swore it was haunted. And he was not a guy who got scared easily."

"I wish he were still around to tell us about it," Grace said. She'd had no idea her father had also visited the haunted house. Somehow, knowing they'd had this common experience made her feel closer to him.

"Me too," her mom said, squeezing Grace's arm. "I'll be interested to hear what you find." She stood up and gathered the empty hot cocoa mugs. "I'm going to wash up and head to bed."

Kat stood up so quickly her chair nearly fell over. "Mrs. Levine?" she asked. "Is it all right if Damien and I sleep over? I'm too creeped out to be by myself tonight."

"I don't see why not," Grace's mom said. "As long as you guys call your parents and tell them where you are. I'll make you pancakes in the morning and then we'll go to the historical society office at City Hall."

"The historical society?" Damien asked.

Grace's mom nodded. "I volunteer there some weekends. And haunted or not, that house is a piece of history. If you want to figure out what's really going on there, the historical society is a good place to start."

# CHAPTER 6

Grace led them back to the den. This was usually where they all slept when Kat and Damien stayed over. There was a comfy couch and some beanbag chairs and a computer where Grace did her homework. Grace grabbed some sleeping bags and extra pillows from the closet and set them up—two on the floor and one on the couch.

Kat looked skeptically at the sleeping bags. "I don't know about you guys, but I'm not going to be able to sleep tonight."

"Don't worry," Grace said. "Neither will I. *Damien* could sleep through anything though."

"How are you not creeped out?" Kat asked Damien.

"Of course I'm creeped out," Damien said, "but I grew up with the twins. And if I can sleep through the ruckus that my little brother and sister make, then I can fall asleep anytime, anywhere."

"No going to sleep until we look over everything," Grace said. "I want to make sure we get it backed up on the computer."

Kat shuddered. "I just said I was too scared to sleep. The last thing I want to do is look at more of the stuff that made me scared in the first place. Let's just watch a movie. Something happy and funny."

"C'mon, Kat," Grace pleaded. "Aren't you excited to prove once and for all if the house is haunted or not? This is the part where we actually get to investigate!"

"I think we can safely say that the house is very much haunted," Kat said. "You guys saw the ghost too, don't try to deny it."

"I know you're the least skeptical of us, Kat," Damien said. "But you know we can't just rely on gut feelings to say the place is haunted. Maybe there's a logical way to explain everything we saw and heard."

"Fine," Kat said, turning to Damien. "I will bet you frozen yogurt with all the toppings that we find out the house is haunted."

Betting frozen yogurt had been their friendship tradition ever since they were little. Grace was pretty sure the first frozen yogurt bet had been a competition to see who could learn to ride a bike first. Kat had won that one.

Grace shivered. "Even in October? It's too cold outside to eat cold things."

Damien frowned in mock outrage. "Grace, are you seriously daring to question the frozen yogurt bet?"

She laughed and held up her hands in surrender. "Fine, fine!"

Damien shook hands with Kat. "Agreed. Frozen yogurt says the house *isn't* haunted."

"What about you, Grace?" Kat asked. "Which side are you betting on?"

Grace sighed. "I'm honestly not sure yet. I need to look over what we found." She dug the night vision camera out of her backpack and wiggled the mouse to bring the computer out of sleep mode.

"You can be the neutral judge, then," Damien suggested. "You get to weigh both sides and make the final call on whether Kat is right and the house is haunted, or if I'm right and it's all some sort of hoax."

"Works for me," Grace muttered as she tried to figure out which cable would allow her to upload the video and sound recordings from the devices to their computers.

After several frustrating minutes of installing the ghost hunter software on the desktop computer, Kat's laptop, and Damien's laptop, Grace finally managed to get everything set up.

"Um, Grace?"

Kat's tone worried Grace. "Yeah?"

"I think you still have some cobweb in your hair."

"Ah—gross!" Grace ran her hands through her hair, pulling the cobweb out as quickly as she could. She was about to throw it in the trash, when she stopped to look at it more closely. It didn't feel wispy and sticky like a real spiderweb. It pulled apart like a cotton ball.

"Guys, I think this is fake. Like those bags of cobwebs for Halloween decorations."

"Are you saying the cobwebs in the house's attic were just decorations?" Damien asked.

"Maybe," Grace said. "At least some of them."

Kat raised an eyebrow. "If the cobwebs were fake . . ."

"Then what else was fake?" Damien mused.

"We have a whole lot of evidence to go through," Grace said. "I'll make popcorn."

/////

An hour later, Grace rubbed her eyes, which were dry from staring at the computer screen so intently. She had combed through the video footage frame by frame, but so far, nothing was jumping out at her as definitive proof of a haunting *or* a hoax. They had captured the door slamming shut and the crystal ball glowing and even the appearance of the ghost, but no further clues were revealed.

She looked blearily at her friends. Damien had fallen asleep on the couch, and he now snored softly, his laptop still open and balanced precariously on his legs. Kat sat on the floor with her laptop, leaning against the couch with her eyes closed. At first, Grace thought that Kat had fallen asleep as well, but she realized Kat was just listening to the EVP recordings through her headphones.

Grace was thinking about curling up in her sleeping bag and tackling the investigation after a fresh start in the morning with coffee and pancakes when Kat jumped up with a wordless exclamation.

Damien snorted awake, nearly toppled off the couch, and barely managed to catch himself and the laptop. He sat up smoothly as though nothing had happened, going from fast asleep to wide awake in a split second. "Did you find something, Kat?"

Kat motioned them over, her eyes bright with excitement. "Guys, I heard something on the EVP. Someone was responding to my questions in the sitting room."

"But we didn't hear any responses while we were there," Damien pointed out.

Kat shook her head. "You said it yourself: the whole idea is that the ghosts can't be heard without special equipment. I had to fiddle with the audio settings on this program to get the volume levels right, but there's definitely something weird going on."

"Okay," Damien said. "Let's hear it."

Kat unplugged her headphones and hooked up her laptop to the den's wall speakers. Grace was glad her mom already knew what they were up to and approved, because they were being far from stealthy.

The room filled with the hiss of white noise as Kat played the sound clip. She held a finger to her lips as her own voice came through the speakers.

"Are there any spirits here with us that would like to communicate?" Kat asked on the recording.

Grace had no idea what she expected to materialize out of the wash of static. The sound rose and fell, and Grace tried to not to think about how it sounded like someone breathing.

"I invite you to come talk with us," Kat said on the recording. "We mean you no harm."

"Yeah, we come in peace," they heard Damien say. "Take us to your leader."

Kat's voice continued on the recording. "Do you have a name? What's your name?"

There was a crackle of static on the recording. Kat paused the recording and looked at Grace and Damien. She seemed to be waiting for their reactions.

"Umm, was that it?" Grace asked.

Kat's face fell. "Obviously. Didn't you guys hear it?"

Damien shook his head. "Hear what?"

Kat huffed in frustration and moved the recording back a few seconds. "Really pay attention this time." She cranked up the volume.

"What's your name?" Kat's voice said again, practically booming from the speakers. Grace winced and hoped her mom wasn't trying to sleep.

But then in the burst of static that followed, Grace could hear it. It was like finally seeing the hidden object in a picture. Once spotted, it seemed so obvious that it was hard to believe you had ever missed it in the first place.

"*Cor . . . eel . . . yarose . . .*"

Kat paused the recording again with a smug smile.

"Cordelia Rose," Grace whispered.

Damien's eyes were wide, but he shook his head slowly. "No, I don't buy it. We're only hearing what we expect to hear. It was just a bunch of gibberish and microphone feedback."

Kat scowled at him. "You're just worried you're going to lose the bet."

"Was there anything else on the recording?" Grace asked.

Kat checked the time stamp on the recording. "Yeah, I think there's just the part where you ask for a sign of the ghost's presence and the door slams shut. I haven't listened to that part yet." She clicked play.

This time, Grace's voice came from the speakers. She grimaced. She always felt her voice sounded odd on recordings.

"Can you give us a sign of your presence?"

There was another burst of static and a loud *whump* as the door slammed shut. Damien's recorded shout blasted from the speakers. Grace quickly reached to turn down the computer's volume.

But before she could, a strange voice growled from the speakers, so close and clear that it sounded like it had been only inches away from the recorder.

"*GET . . . OUT . . .*"

# CHAPTER 7

Even in the safety of her family's den, Grace's blood ran cold at the sound of the voice. There had been a lot of commotion after the door slammed shut, but she would have sworn that she hadn't heard any voice at the house.

Even Damien looked shaken. The first response had been garbled and open to debate, but this was crystal clear and unmistakable.

He cleared his throat. "I mean, it's a woman's voice, so I guess skeptics would say that it was one of you two faking it just to mess with me."

Kat scoffed, looking offended. "I would never, *ever* do something like that—"

Before she could go off on a rant about trust and friendship, Grace cut in. "C'mon, Damien, you know what both of us sound like, and that was definitely not my voice or Kat's."

Damien's eyes flicked between the two girls once more before he sighed and nodded. "Okay, okay. You're right." He eyed Kat, who still looked offended. "I'm sorry, jeez!"

"So what do we do now?" Grace asked.

"I think we need more information," Damien said. "We should see if we can look up more details about Cordelia Rose."

"My mom pays for a subscription to one of those ancestry websites," Kat offered up. "I could ask her for her log-in and we could see if we can track down Cordelia Rose's backstory."

Grace yawned and flopped down on the floor in her sleeping bag. "I don't know about you guys, but I say we tackle this in the morning."

Kat and Damien gave weary nods. Grace had thought that after all the things that had happened that day, that she would be kept awake all night. But she fell asleep as soon as her head hit the pillow.

/////

Grace woke with a start, staring foggily at her surroundings. As soon as she remembered why she was sleeping on the floor in the den and not in her own bed, she started to feel more awake. She reached out to grab her glasses before she realized that they were already on her face. *I must have fallen asleep without even taking them off*, she realized.

She looked over at her sleeping friends. Kat and Damien still seemed to be passed out, so Grace trudged to the kitchen in search of coffee.

Her mom was already awake, listening to the public radio station's morning talk show as she poured pancake batter on the electric griddle. After the weirdness of the night before, it was a welcome sight.

"I'm glad you don't keep jars of eyeballs in our kitchen, Mom."

Her mom turned around and gave her an amused half-smile. "Good morning to you too." She flipped the pancakes over, the batter hissing. "And you don't know what I keep in the laundry room," she added with a wink.

Grace laughed. "Is that a hint that I should help you with the laundry?"

"How nice of you to offer!" Her mom grinned jokingly. "So, how's the investigation going?"

Grace poured herself a cup of coffee, enjoying the sharp aroma that rose from her mug in spirals of steam. "We've looked over all the footage, but instead of proving anything, it's just made things more confusing."

"What's your evidence so far?" her mom asked, sliding the pancakes off the griddle.

Grace ticked the items off on her fingers. "One, doors kept slamming mysteriously, although it could have just been the wind. Two, we heard a really creepy voice say 'get out' when we played back the recording. Oh, and three, we actually saw the ghost of Cordelia Rose."

Her mom paused, a pancake balanced on the spatula. "Seriously?"

Grace nodded. "Sorry, I probably should've started with that part. We were too shaken up to tell you last night."

Her mom put a couple of pancakes on a plate and handed it to Grace before grabbing a plate for herself. "Maybe you should start from the beginning."

/////

After Grace had roused Kat and Damien with the offer of pancakes and coffee, the three of them took turns recounting the story for Grace's mom.

"You do believe us, don't you, Mrs. Levine?" Kat asked after they finished.

"Of course! I believe that you really did see those things."

Damien frowned. "So you agree with Kat that the house is actually haunted?"

"Not quite," Grace's mom said as she cleared their plates. "You know *what* you saw, but you don't know *why* you saw it."

"Exactly," Grace chimed in. "There could be a logical explanation for everything." She thought again of the ghost of Cordelia Rose and suppressed a shudder. "Maybe."

Kat seemed to read her thoughts. "But how do you explain the creepy ghost lady?" She raised on arm and pointed at Damien across the breakfast table, twisting her face into a scowl. "Get out!" she said in a spooky wail. Damien wrinkled his nose at her and she grinned mischievously.

Grace rolled her eyes. "Miss Drama Queen is right, though. How do we find a rational explanation for a ghost with glowing eyes?"

"It could have been a trick," Damien pointed out. "Like someone in a costume."

"There is *no* way that was just a costume," Kat said, folding her arms.

"We didn't really get a good look at the ghost though," Grace pointed out. "It was dark and stormy and we were already scared."

"Did you guys still want to stop by City Hall today?" her mom asked. "I usually try to stop by the historical society for a few hours on Saturdays anyway."

"This afternoon," Grace said. "There's something we have to check out first at the house."

"*What?*" Kat looked appalled. "You want to go *back*? Are you serious?"

Grace shrugged. "It's a beautiful morning," she said. "I think that we should go and see what the house looks like when it's not a dark and stormy night."

"Grace has a point," Damien said. "It'll be a lot less creepy when the sun is shining."

Kat groaned as she grabbed her sweatshirt and backpack. "You two will be the death of me."

# CHAPTER 8

In the bright October sunshine under a vibrant blue sky, Grace thought the house seemed lonely, as if it sagged with weariness. It was no longer menacing—more like a predator that had lost its teeth and could no longer bite.

They checked to make sure no one was watching, but once again, Cherry Avenue was empty. As they climbed the creaky steps to the front door, Grace noticed something was missing. "Hey, the candy bowl is gone."

Damien shrugged and pushed the front door open, followed by Kat. Grace couldn't understand why her friends didn't seem to think the candy bowl was an important clue.

The hallway was still stuffy and musty smelling, but now dust danced in beams of weak sunlight that filtered in through the curtains. Grace peeked around the door to the sitting room before she crept inside. Empty. The terror of the night before had been replaced by a feeling of vague unease and melancholy.

Grace pulled one of the lace curtains open, covering her face with her sweatshirt sleeve to protect her mouth and nose from the whirlwind of dust that was kicked up. The windows were still caked with grime, but sunlight streamed into the room. As far as they knew, it was the first time in years that the room had seen the sun.

She turned to see that Kat had followed her into the room, but Damien wasn't with her.

"He went to check out the kitchen," Kat explained, jabbing her thumb over her shoulder toward the hallway. She glanced briefly at Grace as she spoke, but she seemed incredibly absorbed in something on her phone, her brow furrowed in concentration. Grace wanted to know what she was up to but didn't want to interrupt.

Then Kat looked up excitedly from her phone. "I found her!"

Grace raised an eyebrow. "Could I get a little more context on that?"

Kat huffed impatiently and held up her phone. "My mom gave me the log-in to the ancestry app, so I searched for Cordelia Rose, based on the fact that she was around in the 1920s. There's not that many results, but look at the one at the top!"

Grace crowded next to Kat to look at the screen. A glamorous young woman with dark curls stared out at her from a black and white photo. Her eyes were heavily lined with dark makeup, and she wore a headband with beaded fringe.

"Well, she certainly looks like a medium," Grace said.

Kat read selections from the bio provided on the app. "It says here that she was born in New York City as Mabel Carter. Cordelia Rose is the stage name she chose when she began to hold séances and became a world-famous medium. You were right about the Houdini bit! It says Houdini was convinced she was a fake and it ended up destroying her career."

Grace's eyes had caught something farther down the page. "Hold on," she muttered. "Oh! Ummm . . ."

Kat leaned in closer to the phone. "What is it?"

Grace pointed out a line in the bio. "It says that Cordelia Rose performed exclusively in New York City. She never left."

Kat's eyes were wide. "But that means—"

"There's no mention of Mason Falls," Grace concluded. "Cordelia Rose was real, but she never lived in this house."

"Then who did live here? How did we see the ghost of Cordelia Rose?"

Grace hit the app's back button to look at the other search results further down in the list. "Wait a second, there's another Cordelia Rose from around the same time period. Cordelia Rose Callaghan. *She* was born in Mason Falls."

"So a woman named Cordelia Rose lived here, but not the Cordelia Rose we thought it was?" Kat massaged her temples. "I never thought this would be so complicated!"

Damien rushed into the room carrying a jar of eyeballs.

Grace looked from the eyeballs and back to Damien, her mouth hanging slightly open, at a loss for words.

Damien grinned. "They're not real!"

"How on Earth can you tell?" Kat asked, looking as though she might be sick.

"Well, I was exploring the kitchen, and I noticed that the jars smelled like lemon-lime." He unscrewed the lid, in spite of Kat's loud protests and mock gagging. Grace cautiously leaned in a little closer. Damien was right. It really did smell like lemon-lime drink mix.

Grace frowned. "But—"

"And that's when I noticed that the eyeballs all look the same and they all have green irises. What are the chances?"

"Uhh—"

"So I picked one of them up—"

"What?" Kat squeaked. "Eww, please tell me you didn't—"

"And it turns out they're just rubber bouncy balls!" And before Grace or Kat could protest, he had plucked an eyeball out of the jar and thrown it to the floor.

It bounced.

"It's like the cotton cobwebs—" Damien started.

Kat gasped. "Do you think it's *all* fake?"

Damien nodded. "I think that someone set this up to make everyone think the house is really haunted. It's an elaborate hoax to scare people away from this place."

"But it's just some creepy old house," Kat said. "Why would someone go to so much trouble to keep people away?"

Suddenly, she hurried past them and disappeared into the hallway. They could hear her pounding up the stairs. Grace looked at Damien, who shrugged, and they followed Kat to see what she was up to.

"I'm in here, guys!" she called from Cordelia Rose's bedroom at the end of the hall.

Kat had dragged one of the chairs from the séance table over to the wall and was leaning against the huge wooden wardrobe, wobbling dangerously. Damien steadied the chair so she could hop down safely. She showed them the picture she had just taken on her phone.

"It's a hidden speaker!" she exclaimed.

Grace could see a tiny black box wedged between the back of the wardrobe and the wall.

"I bet there's more of them all over the place," Kat said.

"That would explain that terrible shrieking noise we heard before the ghost showed up," Grace said. "It was just a haunted house sound effect."

Kat lifted the edge of the heavy embroidered cloth covering the séance table. Underneath, they could see neatly bundled wires and cords that ran from the wall to the crystal ball on the table. Kat flicked a switch, and the crystal ball glowed bright blue.

"But what about the possessed séance table?" Grace asked. "How do we explain that?"

Damien knelt down and examined the table legs. "There's some sort of metal mechanism on each table leg. I bet they can raise and lower each leg at different times so the whole table starts to shake."

Grace folded her arms. She felt creeped out that someone would play such a cruel trick on them. "Do you think it was Hector and Chrissy?" she asked.

Kat snorted. "They're way too dumb to pull off something like this."

"We better head over to City Hall and tell my mom what we found," Grace said. "She's going to want to hear this."

Back in the hallway, Grace paused suddenly. "I have an idea," she explained. "Wait a sec."

"Where are you going?" Kat called after her.

Grace didn't answer. When she reached the end of the hall farthest away from Cordelia Rose's bedroom, she tried the door that had been locked the night before. The lock rattled as she tried to force it open. Frustrated, she wondered if it was really possible to pick a lock with a bobby pin. Then she realized the obvious answer to her problem.

She hurried back down the hallway, running past her confused friends. Once back in Cordelia Rose's bedroom, Grace headed for the balcony where they had seen the ghostly figure. These doors opened easily. When she thought back to the ghost's dramatic entrance the night before, Grace wondered if these doors were hooked up to some sort of mechanism as well. That would explain how they had burst open at just the right moment.

From the balcony, Grace had a good view of Cherry Avenue. She could see her house on the corner. She could also see that the balcony extended along the front of the house and a second set of glass doors connected the balcony to another room.

Grace breathed a sigh of relief when she found that the doors on this side of the room were unlocked. The room was smaller and barer than Cordelia Rose's bedroom. There were no tapestries or lace curtains. Everywhere else was coated in what looked like decades of dust, but this room was spotless. A toolbox, a tub labeled *Prop Dust*, and several bags of Halloween candy were lined up neatly along the wall.

A flapper dress made of shimmering pale green fabric hung from a hook on the wall. Grace ran a hand over the intricate designs embroidered with gold thread and sequins. The glass beads in the dress's fringe clinked together. Grace found a tag sewn on the inside of the dress that said *Mason Falls Community Theater*.

A camp chair was set up at an old-fashioned vanity dresser strewn with strings of fake pearls and the heavy cream makeup that Grace had seen Kat use for theater productions. It was clear that someone had recently used this room to change into a ghost costume. Someone who was very much alive.

Grace could hear the muffled shouts of her friends from the hallway, and she was about to unlock the hallway door to show them what she had found when she noticed a second door in the corner. It opened silently. A narrow, steep set of stairs descended into the pitch-black stairwell. She fumbled along the wall and found a light switch. Small lights along the base of the wall gave a faint golden glow that was enough to see by. Grace crept down the steps and pushed open the door at the bottom. She was surprised to find herself in the kitchen. She hadn't noticed this door in the corner when it had been dark.

She crept down the hallway to the front stairs and called up to her friends. "Are you guys coming or not?"

She was rewarded by a shriek of surprise from Kat and some muttered exclamations from Damien. Grace tried not to laugh.

Her friends appeared at the top of the stairs.

"How did you get down *there*?" Kat asked.

Grace grinned. "It turns out there's a second staircase at the back of the house. It leads from the kitchen to the locked room upstairs. And then the balcony stretches from the locked room to the bedroom."

"Well, that explains how our 'ghost' was able to move around so easily without us seeing her," Damien said.

Grace took them upstairs and showed them what she had found.

"Weird," Damien said. "This must be the base of operations."

Kat grimaced. "Let's get out of here."

"Okay," said Grace. "But we're not done investigating. I still want to find out who's doing this."

Kat shuddered. "What sort of creep hangs around an abandoned house just to scare people? They really need some new hobbies."

# CHAPTER 9

At City Hall, they met Grace's mom in the break room. Not many people worked there on Saturdays, but her mom and a few other volunteers stopped in every couple of weekends to help out when they could.

She looked shocked to hear about the elaborate setup at the house. "Wow," she said. "I always figured it wasn't really haunted, but I never imagined someone would fake a haunting."

"Why was there a hidden stairwell, anyway?" Kat asked.

Grace's mom answered, "In the past, large houses often had two sets of stairs—one in the front of the house for family members, and one in the back of the house for servants. That way, servants could come and go without running into their employers or their guests."

"I bet that's why the one we discovered led into the kitchen," Grace said excitedly. "But what about the small room at the top?"

"Probably a servant's bedroom," her mom mused. "But I'd have to see it for myself to know for sure."

"You don't want to go anywhere near that creepy place, Mrs. Levine," Kat said, shaking her head vigorously.

"But we know now that it's not really haunted," Damien said. "Which, by the way, means you still owe me frozen yogurt with all the toppings. I was right."

Kat wrinkled her nose at Damien. "Yeah, but just because I lost doesn't mean that the house is safe. We still need to figure out who's doing this and why."

Grace suddenly had an idea. "Mom? Would City Hall have a record of who used to live in that house? We know that someone named Cordelia Rose lived there in the 1920s—"

"But *not* the famous medium named Cordelia Rose," Kat interjected. "Just some other woman with the same name."

"Ah," Grace's mom said. "That would explain how the legend got started—"

"But," Grace continued, "we don't know who lived there more recently. I bet someone else lived there after Cordelia Rose. I doubt the house has been abandoned for almost a century."

Her mom pursed her lips thoughtfully. "I think I know where I can find that info in the City Hall database. I'm not sure how long it will take me to find it, though."

"That's fine," Grace said, looking at her friends. "Just call me when you have an update. I know exactly what we need to do in the meantime."

/////

"I still don't get what this has to do with the house," Kat said as they leaned their bikes against the low stone wall that surrounded the cemetery.

“I want to see if the real Cordelia Rose was buried here,” Grace explained. “The one who actually used to live in the house. Her bio on that website said she never left Mason Falls.”

They walked into the cemetery.

“It’s weird being in a cemetery this close to Halloween,” Damien said, pulling his sweatshirt sleeves over his hands as the wind picked up. Even with the sun shining, it was clear that winter wasn’t far off.

As they searched the headstones for the right name, Grace’s gaze strayed over to the shade-dappled corner where her dad’s grave was. Tomorrow, she and her mom would stop by to place a jack-o’-lantern on his headstone like they did every year. Grace smiled at the thought. Halloween had always been her dad’s favorite holiday.

Toward the back of the cemetery, where the dates stretched back to the earliest days of Mason Falls, they found the headstone of Cordelia Rose Callaghan under an oak tree.

They stared quietly at the headstone for a few moments until Grace, suddenly beginning to feel self-conscious, pushed her glasses up her nose and decided to continue looking around. Kat and Damien split off as well, heading down different rows.

Grace was surprised to see a headstone with Cordelia Rose's last name on the stone next to hers. "Hey, look at this," she called to the others. They came to stand next to her. "Looks like she was married."

"Peter Callaghan," Kat read.

"And look," Damien said, pointing to the headstone next to the couple's. "Robert Callaghan—look at the dates. I bet he was their son."

Grace's phone buzzed in her back pocket and she flushed, wondering if it was inappropriate to answer a phone call in a cemetery. But the caller ID said it was her mom, so she stepped away from the graves and answered.

"Hey, Mom. What'd you find?"

"Well, I had to dig through the files and ask a favor from a friend at City Hall, but I got the info you're looking for."

Grace put the phone on speaker and motioned Kat and Damien over to listen.

"Cordelia Rose Callaghan died after her husband, and the house passed to their son."

"Robert," Kat answered.

" . . . yes," Grace's mom said, sounding surprised. "How did you know that?"

"We're, uh . . ." Grace looked over at Kat and Damien, who shrugged. "We're at the cemetery. We found Cordelia Rose's grave. Her husband has a headstone here, and her son too."

"What else did you find?" Damien asked, bringing them back to the topic at hand.

"Well," her mom continued, "after that, it looks like the house was passed on to Robert's daughter—Shirley McCall."

"McCall?" Kat repeated, a thoughtful look crossing her face. "Why does that name sound so . . . oh!" She rushed over to a headstone a row ahead of the Callaghan family. "Here!"

Damien and Grace followed, where they saw a newer headstone with the name *Douglas McCall* on it.

"Mom, is Douglas McCall Shirley's husband?" Grace asked.

"One minute." They could hear her typing through the phone. While they were waiting, Damien pulled out his own phone and started swiping at the screen. Finally, Grace's mom said, "Yes—Douglas and Shirley McCall were married. Hm, that's strange."

"What?"

"The house has been in Shirley's name for nearly fifty years—no one else is associated with it. But I don't remember anyone ever living in there. I wonder if she's still the current owner."

"Well, she's not buried here with the rest of the family," said Grace. "Maybe she's still alive." *And maybe she's our fake ghost.*

Damien raised his phone in excitement. "I found her! Shirley McCall lives at Golden Meadows Assisted Living Apartments, here in Mason Falls."

"Damien," Grace's mom said, "I don't even want to know how you found that information."

He flushed. "It's the magic of the Internet, Mrs. Levine!" Kat and Grace laughed.

"I wonder if she'd be willing to talk to us," Grace said.

"Grace," her mom cut in, "I know I can trust you to do the right thing here. You can see if she'll give you the answers you're after, but be respectful. And be careful."

# CHAPTER 10

Grace hesitated briefly in front of the main doors at Golden Meadows. Then she pushed the intercom button labeled *Shirley McCall* on the panel next to the entrance. She had no idea what to expect. What sort of person spent their free time dressing up as a ghost and scaring people away from an abandoned house?

The intercom crackled. "Yes? Can I help you?"

"Hi, Mrs. McCall, my name is Grace and I'm here with my friends Kat and Damien. And, umm, we're here to talk to you about the house on Cherry Avenue."

There was no response, and for a moment Grace worried that they would be turned away.

"We know about Cordelia Rose and Mabel Carter," she added.

"I knew someone would figure it out eventually," Mrs. McCall said. "I think you kids better come in. Apparently we have a lot to discuss."

There was a buzzing sound and they heard the door latch click open.

The apartment was small and simply furnished, designed for easy mobility and comfort. A small electronic dial pad near the door had buttons labeled with various nurses, emergency providers, and services like cleaning. Mrs. McCall had decorated for Halloween, with elegant arrangements of spray-painted gold pumpkins and black lace cloth draped like spider webs.

Mrs. McCall wore a deep red dressing gown and had steel gray hair, cut short in a stylish bob. Her face was crisscrossed with fine lines like crumpled tissue paper and she leaned on a cane to support herself, but her eyes were bright and alert.

She carefully lowered herself into an armchair. She placed her cane on the end table next to her tablet and tissue box. "I'm sorry I don't have a snack to offer you," she said, gesturing toward the apartment's tiny kitchen. "But I'm afraid I'm getting most of my meals in the community dining room these days."

"That's fine, Mrs. McCall," Grace said as she and Kat and Damien sat down on the couch. "We're just excited to get to meet you face-to-face."

Mrs. McCall stared at them intently for a long moment. "You're the three who were at the house on Friday night, aren't you?" She chuckled. "You lasted a lot longer than most kids do. It's not often that I have to break out the full ghost ensemble. And it's getting harder to do the full performance these days." She glanced meaningfully at the cane beside her.

"But *why* are you dressing up like Cordelia Rose and pretending to haunt the place?" Grace asked. "We can tell that you want to scare people away, but what does that accomplish?"

Mrs. McCall smiled wryly. "It doesn't look like much nowadays, but let me tell you, that used to be the most beautiful house in all of Mason Falls. My grandfather built it when he moved here and met his wife."

"Who just happened to have the same name as a famous medium," Grace added.

Mrs. McCall blushed. "Yes, that came in handy when I needed to save the house."

"What do you mean, save the house?" asked Damien.

"Well, I inherited the place eventually. My husband and I were hoping to move in there after my parents left town, but around the same time I lost my Doug to cancer."

She paused, and Grace thought she could see a tear clinging to her eyelashes. "All the medical bills left me pretty short on money. And a house as big and old as that one needs a lot of expensive upkeep. I couldn't afford all the maintenance it would take to keep the place livable. But I also couldn't bear to lose a place that meant so much to me and to three generations of my family."

Mrs. McCall sighed and closed her eyes, pinching the bridge of her nose. "And then I started hearing from developers who wanted to buy the lot and knock down the house to build a gas station."

"That's awful!" Kat exclaimed.

"I certainly thought so. But I started to worry about what would happen after I'm gone. I don't have any family now—no one to inherit the property. It'll probably go to the bank when I die."

"And you were afraid the bank would sell it to developers who'd tear the house down," Damien finished for her.

"So you started the rumor that the famous Cordelia Rose used to live there?" Grace guessed.

Mrs. McCall gave a sheepish smile. "My grandmother was an amazing woman, but she didn't have quite the same element of drama and mystery that a medium from New York does. Once the people who actually knew her had all passed on, it was easy enough for me to convince folks that Grandma was actually the famous Cordelia Rose. I don't have developers calling me every other day anymore. No one wants to build on haunted property. I hope that'll still be true after I pass on."

"So you've been haunting the place single-handedly all these years?" Kat asked in a hushed voice.

Mrs. McCall nodded. "It's not all bad though. I always make a point of leaving out candy for trick-or-treaters every year around Halloween, just like I used to do when I still lived there." She massaged her knee and winced. "I don't think I'll be able to keep up with the hauntings for much longer though. My knee is acting up from going up and down the back staircase on Friday night."

"How were you able to create such elaborate special effects?" Damien asked. "Like the hidden speakers and the mechanism that shook the table."

Mrs. McCall laughed in surprise. "You kids are smarter than some of the adults I've scared. I used to work as an engineer before I retired, which is how I managed to rig up some of those contraptions. I also helped with lights and stage crew at the community theater. That's where I picked up some tricks that helped me put together the Cordelia Rose costume and ghost makeup."

"But what about the ghost's glowing eyes?" Kat asked, leaning forward until she was perched on the edge of her seat.

"LED lights attached to an eye mask," Mrs. McCall explained. "It wouldn't hold up to close inspection, but most people don't stick around long enough to find out."

Grace had been mulling something over as they talked, and a plan was beginning to take shape. She would have to discuss it with Kat and Damien, and it would take them the rest of the day to set in motion, but it seemed like it really had a chance of working.

She stood up, ignoring the puzzled looks that Kat and Damien gave her. It was time to let Mrs. McCall get some rest anyway. It looked like her knee was paining her.

"Thank you so much for your time, Mrs. McCall. If it's all right, we'd like to come back tomorrow and visit again. A special Halloween treat."

Mrs. McCall smiled warmly. "Halloween was always my favorite holiday."

# CHAPTER 11

The next evening, after a day and a half of hard work on the secret project, Grace, Kat, and Damien returned to Golden Meadows. Grace had opted for cat ears and a black turtleneck and skirt like she usually did, and Damien was dressed as a mad scientist, complete with a frazzled white wig and a lab coat. Kat had borrowed a few items from their high school's costume department and gone as a flapper, in honor of Cordelia Rose.

A few of the residents had put out candy, but the halls were empty of children. The three of them trick-or-treated their way to Mrs. McCall's room, and the residents seemed delighted that their efforts were appreciated.

Mrs. McCall's face lit up when she saw them. "I wasn't sure you were going to stop by after all." She was dressed as a witch, with a black pointy hat, but instead of robes, she had a glamorous black dress trimmed with silver lace.

Grace was barely able to contain her excitement. "Can we show you something?"

/////

Grace, Kat, and Damien crowded around Mrs. McCall's chair as she opened the program they had installed on her tablet.

Kat used her hands to make a drum roll sound on her legs. "Introducing Mason Falls' first remote operated, entirely automated haunted house!"

Grace selected the camera symbol from the app menu. Multiple camera views of the inside and outside of the house appeared on the screen.

Mrs. McCall leaned forward. "My goodness," she said quietly.

"We took all of the haunted special effects that you've installed and wired them so that you can control them from this app," Grace explained.

Damien pointed to the other symbols in the app's menu. "You can control the shaking table and the slamming doors from here. You also have access to a variety of spooky sound effects, lighting schemes, and music tracks."

"And just wait until you see how we automated the ghost effect!" Kat said, bouncing up and down on the balls of her feet.

Mrs. McCall's lips quavered as she smiled. "This is just wonderful! I've always wondered if it was possible to set up something like this, but computer tech was only just coming around when I studied engineering."

Movement on the security camera video feed caught her eye as two kids appeared on the screen. "Who are they?" she asked.

Grace grinned. "They are the test case. These are the kids from our school who originally dared us to spend an hour at the house. We dared them back."

"We told them it was *definitely* haunted and that it was the scariest experience in our entire lives," Kat added.

"We told them we didn't think they could even beat our record of fifty minutes before they ran away, screaming in terror," Damien said, laughing.

They watched as Hector and Chrissy crept up the front steps of the house and slipped inside.

Mrs. McCall was already scanning the menu for options, muttering a plan of attack to herself. She paused and smiled at them, her eyes gleaming mischievously. "How scared do you want them?" she asked.

"Scare the living daylights out of them!" Damien said.

Grace squeezed Mrs. McCall gently on the shoulder and winked. "We'll let you take it from here."

/////

The next day after school, Grace's mom gave them a ride to the frozen yogurt place.

"So, how did the test run of the new system go?" Mrs. Levine asked as they sat down at a table to eat.

"Fantastic!" Damien said around a mouthful of marshmallows, sprinkles, and blueberries.

Grace smirked. "Mrs. McCall told me that Hector and Chrissy didn't even last ten minutes. She said she was actually disappointed that she didn't get to try out all of the bells and whistles."

"I thought you guys wanted to end the dare tradition?" her mom asked.

"We decided that it was more important to protect Mrs. McCall's secret and the legacy of the house," Grace explained. "And besides, now we know that the kids who go there are perfectly safe. We aren't going to force anyone into going in, like the seniors have been doing, but . . ." She gave a mischievous grin. "If people want to check it out, who are we to stop them?"

"Plus Hector and Chrissy have suddenly lost a lot of their enthusiasm for the tradition,"

Damien laughed. "Maybe they'll convince the other seniors to stop too."

Kat chimed in, "We're setting up a website for the house and starting a social media campaign to promote it. We're branding it as the most haunted house in the state, so no one will ever want to buy the property. Or at least if someone does buy it after Mrs. McCall is gone, they won't want to tear down the famous house."

"It's going to be a hit," Damien said. "People love to pretend ghosts are real."

Kat pouted. "Just because the ghost of Cordelia Rose wasn't real, that doesn't mean that ghosts don't exist."

"Mom, didn't you say you had some good news for us?" asked Grace.

Her mom smiled. "The historical society has decided to buy the house and add it to the historic register. It will be a historical landmark, so no one will ever be able to tear it down."

"That's amazing!" Grace said. "Mrs. McCall will be so happy."

“As long as the historical society doesn’t mind us stopping by the house from time to time,” added Damien.

“Right,” said Grace, “because we promised Mrs. McCall that we would put out candy for trick-or-treaters every year. A tradition that’s definitely worth carrying on!”

Kat launched into explaining her ideas for promoting the website—most of which involved flash mobs with song-and-dance numbers. Meanwhile Damien tried to explain to Grace’s mom how he was going to track the website’s popularity.

While her friends chattered, Grace ate her frozen yogurt and stared out the shop window, lost in thought. It was a beautiful November morning that still clung to the last of October, with a crisp blue sky and the rustle of fiery-orange leaves.

She smiled.

This had always been her favorite time of year.

# MASON FALLS MYSTERIES

BEHIND THE SCREEN
THE HOUSE
TRACKS
THE TURNAROUND

EVEN AN ORDINARY TOWN
HAS ITS SECRETS.

# DAY OF DISASTER

*Would you survive?*

# ABOUT THE AUTHOR

Raelyn Drake lives in Minneapolis, Minnesota, with her husband (who lovingly tolerates her obsession with mysteries) and rescue corgi mix, Sheriff (who isn't afraid of any ghosts).